# CLANCY WITH THE PUCK

written and illustrated

by Chris Mizzoni

**RAINCOAST BOOKS**
*www.raincoast.com*

**STUDIO B PRODUCTIONS**

Raincoast Books gratefully acknowledges the financial support of the Province of
British Columbia through the BC Arts Council and the Book Publishing Tax Credit
and the Government of Canada through the Canada Council for the Arts, and the
Book Publishing Industry Development Program (BPIDP).

ZAMBONI and the configuration of the Zamboni(r) ice resurfacing machine
are registered trademarks of Frank J. Zamboni & Co., Inc.

Writing and editorial contributions by Tonya Martin, Lisa Mervyn,
        Grenfell Featherstone
Illustration contributions by Cathy Matusicky
Cover and interior design by Candace Sepulis

Cataloguing in Publication available from Library and Archives Canada

Raincoast Books
9050 Shaughnessy Street
Vancouver, British Columbia
Canada  V6P 6E5
www.raincoast.com

Printed in China.

10 9 8 7 6 5 4 3 2 1

Acknowledgements

Special thanks to my parents Pat and Linda, and my dad for taking me to
opening night, 1981, at Maple Leaf Gardens, one of my first and greatest hockey
memories.  Thanks to all the great people at Raincoast Books who believed in
this project. Thanks to Blair, Chris and Rob at Studio B Productions for getting
behind and supporting my initial idea.

The author consulted the following reference materials:
Books by these authors: Roch Carrier and Ernest Lawrence Thayer.
Hockey Cards: O-Pee-Chee and Parkhurst  hockey cards from the 1950s–1970s.

To my two lovely girls,
Dreya and Nancy

**Hockey** was the game for Clancy Cooke:
he could skate and shoot and win.

As a boy at the rink, he was on display;
all eyes were turned on him.

He'd look up and wave during breakaways,
blowing kisses to the girls.

Once he'd scored,
he'd stop to flirt and brush his flowing curls.

The lowly Hogtown Maple Buds
were a sorry, desperate team.

They played like a tractor:
old and slow,
they were not lean and mean.

The Stanley Cup?
They had no hope
that they would win that season,

Until young Clancy was traded in,
and then they had a reason.

Clancy skated like the wind;
he scarcely touched the ground.

Each time he went to slap the puck,
a cannon shot would sound.

When Clancy scored the winning goal
to secure their play-off spot,

The fans rejoiced in Clancy's deed:
they finally had their shot.

The rink was packed
for the final Cup match;
the teams took to the ice.

As time ticked by, the Buds scored once,
the visitors scored thrice.

HOGTOWN 1
VISITORS 3

HOGTOWN 3
VISITORS 3

Then Clancy fired a pair of goals;
the Buds thought they could win.

HOGTOWN 3
VISITORS 4

But the puck was intercepted;
the opposition slipped one in.

Three goals to four with seconds left;
the defence was changing lines —

Mackenzie got a break-away and
raced down the empty ice.

He then sped in alone on goal,
but the defender raised his stick.

Mackenzie fell, and the whistle blew
to penalize the trip.

TWEEEEET!

Mackenzie writhed upon the ice:
his knee was twisted badly.

The fans went wild up in the stands;
they screamed and hollered madly.

The fans all threw their hats in the air,
their hopes no longer dim.

The lights, the crowd, the refs, the teams,
all turned their eyes on him.

Theatrically he raised his head as if to say, "Who, me?"
Then took to the ice, with a blush of pride,
as if reluctantly.

As he skated slowly around the rink,
his lips grew tight and mean.

The fans went wild;
they called his name—
but Clancy was in a dream.

He saw himself with arms raised up:
the Stanley Cup he held.

The fans in adoration cheered and hollered,
sang and yelled.

His skill and speed and mighty shot
were not matched by any man,

The instant that he scored this goal,
his legend would sweep the land.

But Clancy's dream was broken
when the referee's whistle blew,

And as he glided toward the line,
he knew just what to do.

He bowed once more to all his fans;
the goalie shook in dread.

Clancy strode across the ice;
the crowd roared overhead.

He grimaced at the other bench,
he snickered at the goalie.

He posed and strutted around the ice
to savour the moment slowly.

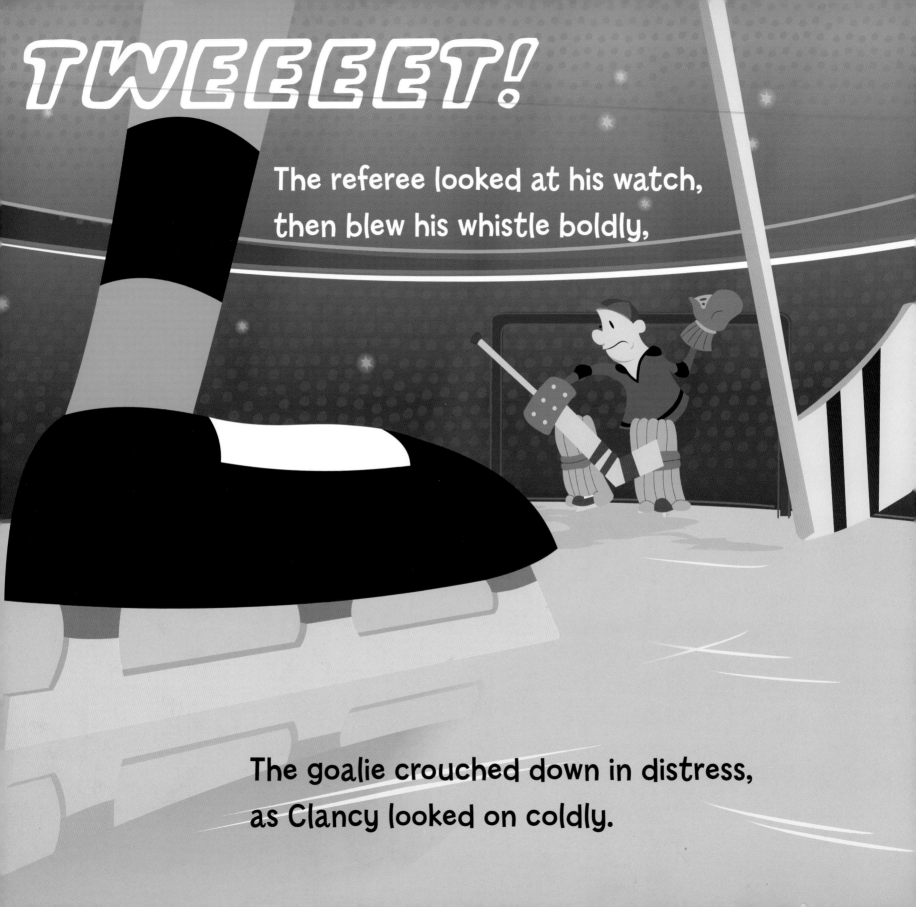

**TWEEEET!**

The referee looked at his watch,
then blew his whistle boldly,

The goalie crouched down in distress,
as Clancy looked on coldly.

Clancy weaved from side to side as
he approached his padded foe,

Down came his stick with fearsome might,
a blur of puck and snow.

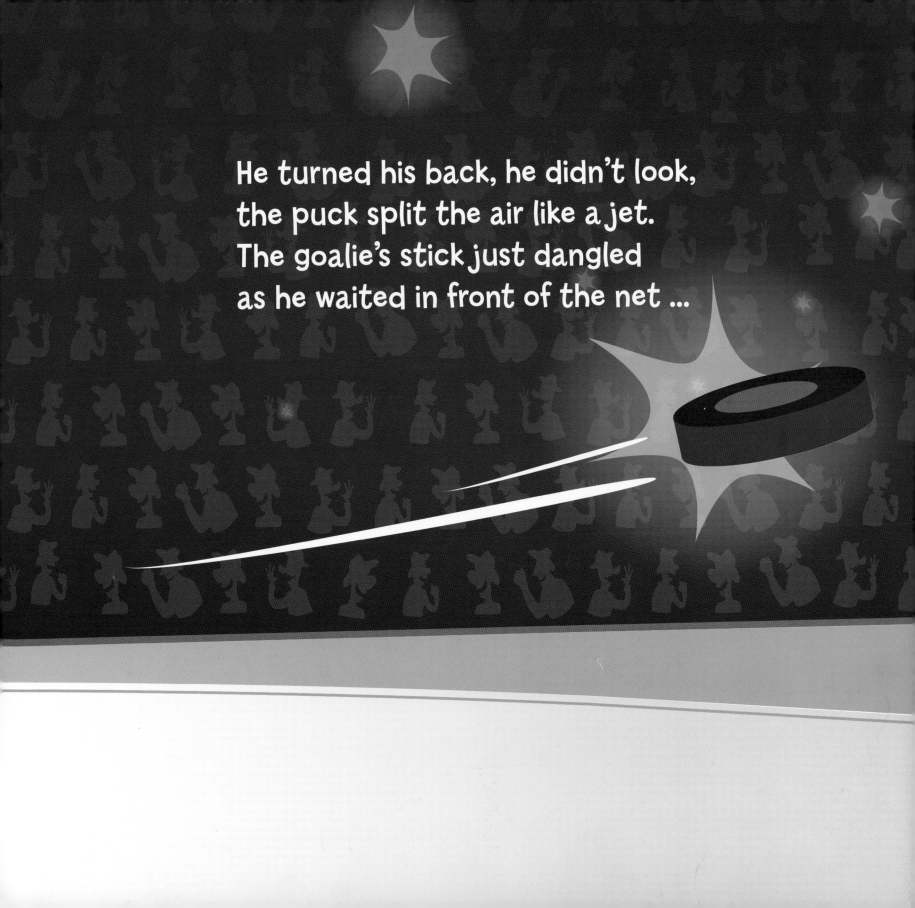

He turned his back, he didn't look,
the puck split the air like a jet.
The goalie's stick just dangled
as he waited in front of the net ...

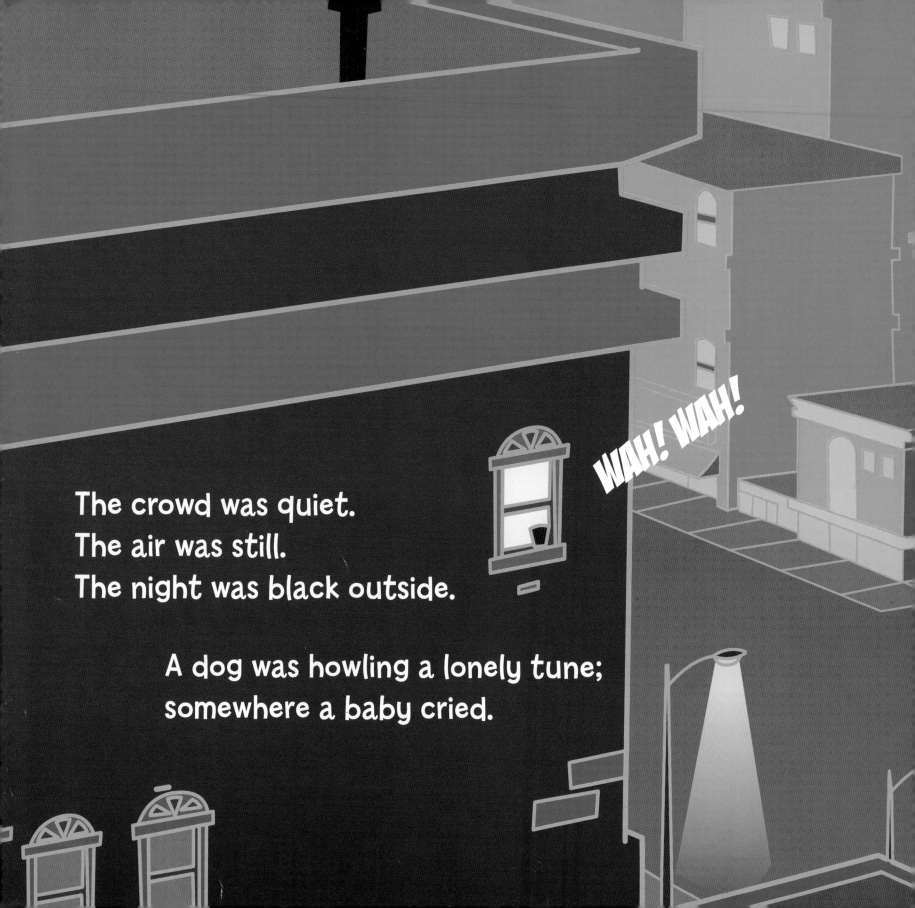

The Buds had lost the Stanley Cup
— and the fans went home to cry.

Old Clancy's not far from the rink these days;
his hands still brush his curls.

He proudly drives the Zamboni now
and waves to all the girls.